ARE EMAILS HOTTER THAN SEX?

SEX IN THE 21ST CENTURY

I0538754

A NOVEL

ELAINE FEUER

Sex in the 21st Century

Author's Note & Copyright

Sex in the 21st Century: Are Emails Hotter Than Sex, is a fictional account of dating, including Internet dating, and its effects on sexuality. It makes no recommendations. As such, the author and publisher disclaim responsibility based on opinions contained herein.

ISBN # 978-0-9634791-7-4

Blue Danube Publishing

Printed in the United States of America

First Printing

To order additional books, or to contact the author:

elaine@elainefeuer.com

http://www.bluedanubepublishingelainefeuer.com

Contents

Chapter One

Our Sexual Marathon

Gloria sends an email to her close friend, Pam:

OMG! OMG! OMG!

It was a sexual marathon! I'm feeling so relaxed right now! This was the first time we've seen each other, other than having dinner last week, since high school, and it was as if we never skipped a beat. It was stunningly passionate!

He picked me up at about 5:00pm on Friday, and we were at his house about ten minutes later. We had cocktails with cheese and crackers; then we had great sex; then we smoked a joint (hash); and then we went into the hot tub – which was wonderful!

For dinner, David made a Caesar salad with chicken. Then we ingested more liquor and made love again, and it was fabulous! He fell asleep and I went into another bedroom, since he snores. I went back into bed with him early Saturday morning and we had sex again! Then he scrambled eggs, adding grated cheese and onions, followed by a drive around the city, including a short walk in a park. We stopped at a tavern for cocktails, and then we went back to his house for more exhilarating sex – followed by panini sandwiches – which were delicious. We smoked another joint, sipped on cocktails, and had phenomenal sex again! Then we lay together in each other's arms. For dinner, he made a salmon salad – and believe it or not – we had more sex before going to sleep! I slept for a little while in bed with him, and then I went back into the other bedroom, again. Early Sunday morning, I joined him in his bed, and this time we had the most electrifying **sex – better than all the other times!** We lay in each other's arms for a while, and then he poached eggs, before driving me back to my hotel, at about noon. His son was coming to stay with him for the upcoming week. He and his ex-wife share custody, every other week.

It was so spectacular, that I'm wondering if it was an illusion or a fantasy! You know, I thought I would never have great sex again, after my divorce, but my mother had told me: "You were part of it, too!" This sex was the best I've ever had – EVER! We had so much fun, in all kinds of positions. OMG! It was a sexual marathon!

Pam:

Wow! I am laughing so hard and I'm jealous! It sounds like you had an extreme weekend. I am so glad it went well and you are both connecting on every level, for the first time since high school. How great! It is so amazing, when you have those feelings again, after thinking you never would. I am very happy for you. It's about timing and I think this was perfect.

Gloria:

Yes, you are correct. There's a reason for everything. **What's astonishing, is that it didn't matter that it's been twenty years since we last saw each other. I know it sounds over-the-top, but there's a trust between us and that's what made the sex so great,** as we cuddled and laughed and argued about who remembers what/where/when during high school.

When I came back to the hotel, I was so exhausted I fell asleep for over an hour, and I never fall asleep, like that. And, I wanted him with me again, for more sex! It was almost too good to be real – I know!

Pam:

I feel it is a blessing for both of you. This will ground you so you can finish your paintings for the art show. I can feel your happiness.

Gloria:

Oh – I didn't tell you, but the hot tub is outside. So when we went outside in our bathing suits, the air was freezing – it was about forty degrees. He massaged my legs in the Jacuzzi, which felt sensational, and when we came out of the hot tub – the cold air felt warm.

Pam:

It sounds like you two were creating your own heat. LOL!

Gloria:

Yes! I'm still smiling today! And I'm still exhausted! I just had a coke to perk me up so that I can finish the painting I told you about. Pam, I can't stop smiling and thinking about it – it was THAT GREAT. It was phenomenal!

Pam:

You should be tired. It's like running the NYC Marathon without training for it. Great sex uses every muscle in your body; even your eyeballs twitch when you have an orgasm. You should be tired but I bet it's a good tired.

Gloria:

My muscles are aching from all the action, that's for sure! But I'm still smiling...

Pam:

It would be the same if you played tennis all day and all night, after not playing for several months. You probably have so much lactic acid built up in your muscles, that it will take a day or two to get rid of it. One thing you can do is eat one half cup of yogurt and one half cup of blueberries, after this type of activity, and it will help the lactic acid dissipate more quickly. I am laughing so hard! I'd love to be in that situation with someone I really cared about!

Gloria Sends an Email to David

"I feel so relaxed and happy. It was fabulous spending the weekend with you. Well, you exhausted me: I fell asleep for more than an hour, as soon as you dropped me off at my hotel. And that never happens to me! I've never "napped" in my entire life! You can put me to sleep anytime! When I first went to bed, I was wearing a warm, white Victoria Secret house coat, and I was imagining having sex with you. I wanted it again – had you been here! I think I would let you do almost anything to me. Do you make house calls? And, you are also an excellent cook. Your ex-wife is insane!"

Gloria to Pam:

He hasn't answered my emails, except for one – but he works from 8:30am – 4:30pm. I think he picks up his son from school, and then he makes dinner. You told me not to expect much – which I certainly understood – but this was above and beyond anything I could have imagined. I'll find a "live" guy for you! Also, each time we had sex, it was for a one hour minimum, and several times, it seemed closer to two hours – no wonder my muscles and ligaments are inflamed! Another endearing moment: In the hot tub, he told me I have "beautiful breasts" and "great legs." I was thinking that I must have looked better in high school, but he's surprised that I haven't gained weight, which is a bit baffling. Back to the present: I've never had so many orgasms in my life, from all sorts of things he was doing, with various parts of my body! Never in my life would I have thought this was attainable after my divorce – never! OMG! OMG! OMG!

Pam:

Sounds good to me! I am so happy to know that you are finally having some fun. He is good for you.

Gloria:

Yes he is!

Two Days Later

Gloria to Pam:

He answered one of my emails yesterday. But don't you think he should have emailed or called? I wonder if this relationship is going to be too distracting for me. You know, I'm already deliberating why he hasn't talked to me since Sunday. On the other hand, while he has his son with him every other week, I can paint. We can be together when his son is with his ex-wife. Am I being too sensitive? I just called him and he acted like he was talking to anyone – and he was watching a TV show, so he wasn't working. Perhaps this isn't a good idea, having an affair with him. Should I do nothing? Or should I email him, asking why he's so blasé? Or should I do the same to him: If he calls, act blasé. If he emails, don't answer him right away. Now I'm starting to be upset and even a little angry. I can't fathom how he could be so loving when I was with him, and now: NOTHING! I called him, and here's what I said, because I don't have time to be upset; it's too distracting:

"I don't understand you. We had a couple of great days together – and now you are totally blasé about it. It was as if I was talking to the Fuller Brush Man. I don't expect you to answer all my emails, since I write a lot of them and you don't, but it sounded as if I was talking to a stranger, when I called you, earlier. Was it just about the sex and nothing else? I've had relationships that are only about the sex. But with you and me, after knowing each other so well, all those years ago, we picked up from where we left off, despite not seeing each other for twenty years."

Pam:

I think you need to let him take the lead and make the next contact. Just like you told me. Men get overwhelmed if a woman comes on too strong at first. I know you know this, but sometimes we need to reinforce it. Play it cool, like you know how to do. Do not let this relationship take over your thoughts. You have the rest of your life and you NEED this Gallery showing to be a success, so get to it. (I mean that in a caring way.) Please let this affair enhance your life but not sidetrack you. So much time and money has been spent, and this will get you on your feet, financially. You want to be coming from a position of power and that will empower you.

The Next Morning

Gloria to Pam:

Here's what David emailed to me this morning:

"It was nice to talk to you last night. I hope you got some rest. I'm not used to getting so many emails from anyone. As far as the content, please bear in mind that I have no privacy when I live with a teenager. I know it was fun for us last weekend, but I don't need to relive it in print."

Here's how I replied to his email:

"I didn't know your son has access to your emails. I also didn't know that you don't receive emails, in general. I send out and receive an abundance of emails – daily, weekly, and so on. It's a fun way to keep up with friends and to know what's happening in other parts of the world. I would not have sent those emails to you, had I known your son has access to them. Have you heard about passwords? You know, last weekend was enchanting and even dream-like: the cocktails and hash helped to make it magical! Since then, we have misinterpreted what the other has said or wrote. I took it personally, when I phoned earlier in the week and you were nonchalant – it was as if you were talking to a stranger. You seem to think that because I sent you emails, that I am looking for a profound relationship.

Almost every divorce is heartbreaking, but you are filled with so much anger and bitterness… I always thought you had this overwhelming brooding quality in high school – but it's even more pronounced today – giving you a "glass half-empty" outlook. I think you need to figure out what will make you happy, before becoming involved in another relationship. The fact that you don't

11

even talk to your ex, while you share custody of a child, is the antithesis to what your son craves. Even if it's just for appearances, you may want to contemplate having some type of a connection with his mother, if only for your son.

I do not intend to be here much longer. I'm attempting to finish my paintings, since I've been inspired living in this lovely hotel. Just being away from home, has been an inspiration.

I thought we could have fun together. Nothing more; nothing less."

Chapter Two

A Summer Romance in New England

Gloria is talking to her friend, Stan:

I've had affairs with married men, because it's safe and I don't feel trapped. I did not want the wives to know; whereas, some of these men took too many chances. Often, it seemed as if they wanted their wives to find out. I am talking about "flings" or summer romances. I've never attempted to break up anyone's marriage. I would never do that.

Stan:

Tell me about Bill.

Gloria:

Bill didn't last very long during sex, and that's an understatement! It felt like thirty seconds the first time, and afterwards, he said: "I didn't think I could last that long!" I couldn't believe it! It happened so fast that I barely felt anything. Yet, we had sex in so many different places: I don't think we had sex in the same place, twice. That's what made our affair so exciting and exhilarating. We also had sex in dangerous places. Bill was always pushing the envelope.

He's the one I had sex with, during the day, on a cot in the supply room, while everyone was at lunch. His wife, Bonnie, could have walked in on us, since she often worked in the office. One morning, Bill asked to see me in his office and he sounded upset, so I was worried that Bonnie had found out about our affair. Instead, he told me he woke up in the middle of the night, because his "penis was on fire." He thought I had an STD. I told him:

"You didn't want to use a condom. I use the sponge, which has spermicide on it, so that's what caused the burning."

Apparently, he planned on paying for an abortion, if I became pregnant. He was relieved and started laughing, and then Bonnie walked into his office. It was rather awkward, since I was standing next to where Bill was sitting, because he had been whispering, before the laughter. Since Bonnie didn't react to me standing so close to Bill, I stayed there for about one minute, before making my escape!

Bill was always touching and kissing me; putting his arm around me; holding my hand in public; kissing me on the lips, across the table in a tavern. I loved it, because he was so affectionate. He also put me on a pedestal. He thought I was perfect and I'm not! He was always commenting on my flat stomach. I would respond: "It should be flat since I haven't had a baby!"

It was the sneaking around that made it so much fun. I worked part-time at his office, while continuing to paint. Bonnie would often complain about Bill to me. I had the impression that their marriage was beyond repair. I would pretend to be attentive when Bonnie was talking, but I never judged or commented on their marriage. They had separated for a couple years, when their kids were quite young; they decided to go back to the marriage, due to the kids. This time, they were attempting to keep the marriage going until their youngest daughter finished high school.

Bill was so attractive and such a Type A personality – although he told me he had calmed down considerably – compared to how he used to be. It was my suspicion that he had women in every part of the country, because he constantly traveled on business. The first time we were about to have sex, I asked him if he had a condom. He seemed bewildered by that question, so I smiled and observed: "Well, you're not exactly a boy scout!" And that extinguished his erection. The next time, we were on his boat – where it was docked – and people could see that Bill was not with his wife. It turned out there was a problem with the boat's motor, so we couldn't take it out. So that was the second time we couldn't have sex. The third time, we finally had sex in a hotel room. You can imagine – given that the first two times had failed – how aroused we were to finally make love. That's when he topped it off by saying he couldn't believe he lasted for so long!

We drank an abundance of liquor, throughout our affair. I can't consume more than two cocktails. That's it. I'm done. I'm floating! Bill could really drink, much more than I could, but then everyone can drink me under the table. He was also an athlete, so you'd think he could have lasted longer during sex. Yet, we had so much fun: having sex in the ocean; on top of the water in his boat; we pulled over on the freeway to have sex in his car; we sipped on drinks and enjoyed dinner at outdoor restaurants – up and down the New England coast. We were in bars and restaurants in downtown Boston, where anyone could have observed that Bill wasn't with his wife. I was more concerned about his wife finding out than he was. We even had sex at his house, when Bonnie was spending one month at their cottage. At first, we were on a couch that opened into a bed, in the family room. Then Bonnie called to check up on him at about 11:00pm, and Bill was so furious, that he made another strong drink for himself, took my hand and said: "Come on!" He took me to their bedroom, and the sheets, the comforter, and the rug, were all in white. I kept worrying about how hard it would be for Bill to catch every one of my long, dark brown hairs. In retrospect, I don't think Bonnie was ever suspicious of me having an affair with her husband. There was an airhead in Seattle, who used their business services, and she was always calling the office to talk to Bill. She was irritating because she was vapid and ridiculous – while clearly being enamored of Bill. I thought they must have had an affair, since he visited Seattle on business, and Bonnie thought so, too. She was beyond angry with Bill, at this point in their marriage, and part of her didn't care if he was having an affair. She was so distant and hostile towards him, that the tension was pervasive throughout the office. There were two other people working there, and one of them was Tony, a close friend of Bill's. Bonnie abhorred him, as well. Tony encouraged our affair because he was separated from his wife and kids. He loved being with Bill – living vicariously through him – since Bill was like "Big" in *Sex and the City* – 100 percent man. Whereas, Tony was effeminate: he loved painting his 6-year-old daughter's nails; and he was dying for his wife to take him back.

I once drove with Bill to New Hampshire, because he wanted to purchase a house, due to the low taxes in that state. Bill introduced me as his wife, to the real estate agent. He was hoping I would live at the house, since I could concentrate on my art instead of worrying about the rent. There was an added incentive: he could visit me whenever he desired, since the house was only an hour's drive from the office.

I thought I needed to get away from Bill, to see if it was the affair I was in love with, instead of Bill. I followed my intuition, instead of choosing the easier financial path. And I turned out to be right, that I was not in love with Bill. I wasn't even sure if I liked him, once I had enough distance from him. He was so good looking and charismatic: when I was in his presence, he had this overwhelming sexual appeal. I was seduced by his magnetic charm.

The last time Bill and I were together, just before I was leaving Massachusetts, we had pizza and a cocktail. I was his heroine: "No man is good enough for you!" Then we went back to his office and he lifted me onto his desk – as the pens and papers went flying! It was a fabulous way to say "good-bye!"

Chapter Three

Condom-Busting Dude!

Stan:

Tell me about that guy in Colorado, who's condoms kept breaking!

Gloria:

This was about having sex for health reasons, and only due to health reasons, since I could not relate to Trevor intellectually, physically, or romantically. We had nothing in common. I was burdened with severe headaches and dizziness, due to the Colorado altitude: it was very hard for me to function. Since I was working on new paintings with specific models, I had to be able to function. I wasn't attracted to Trevor at all, but we would smoke weed, in order for me to be able to have sex with him. I had sex like a guy would: purely for the orgasm. I wouldn't let him kiss me or do anything other than enter me. The funniest part of this affair was that the condoms kept breaking because Trevor had these gargantuan erections – bigger than I have seen in my entire life! I wasn't seduced by his looks or his personality, but the sex curtailed my headaches! Unfortunately, Trevor decided he wanted a "real relationship" with me, and I had to end it, because he kept showing up where I was living. He wanted to be my boyfriend. I told him I was too busy with work to have a relationship with anyone. Thus ended my affair with the gargantuan erections!

Chapter Four

The First Husband

Stan:

So tell me about your first husband? You must have been sexually attracted to Jack, at least that's what I'm assuming!

Gloria:

Of course! That was the reason I lived with him and eventually married him. I met Jack when I was freelancing, since I needed income to support me, while I was a starving artist. I worked in his office off and on for several months, without anyone knowing that we were dating. He had recently separated from his wife, and he asked me out the day after they separated. It was so much fun, surreptitiously, since very few people knew about our affair. I'd stay overnight at his apartment, and then we'd drive our own cars to work. Sometimes, I worked in his office, proof-reading documents. He would often close his door, when I was in there with him. There was an infuriating female employee, who kept barging in because she couldn't stand it, that I was working in Jack's office. We kept our romance a secret for about nine months – it was perfect. I would have been delighted to keep our relationship quiet a little longer, but he wanted people to know we were together.

Stan:

What was it like the first time you had sex with him?

Gloria:

With Jack, the first time we had sex was outstanding, because he could go for so long. I still remember the exact feeling of that first time, when he was inside me. His penis moved slowly and in circular motions. He was in total control, in a way that I had not experienced, before. It was extraordinary, what he could do: it was as if he were playing a Stradivarius and conducting the orchestra! Later, when he was ready to go to sleep, I told him I would probably be leaving, since I didn't think I would be able to fall asleep. He didn't want me walking to my car in the middle of the night, so he stayed up with me. It was fun – we were laughing all night – then I left his apartment at about 7:30am.

We soon made love in all types of positions, for one to two hours. But that first time was astonishing for me. It was comical, a few months later, when he told me he wasn't sure if I enjoyed sex with him, the first time. I deadpanned: "Are you kidding?!" He could have sex anytime and anywhere. And so could I. It was an all-consuming passion between us: an infatuation and addiction to making love; an addiction to pure lust. In hindsight, I doubt I would have stayed with him, if it had not been for the sex. He had so much baggage; whereas, I had none. It was beyond an obsession. It took me almost a year, of not talking to him, to finally be free of our sex mania.

Chapter Five

Fling-Guy!

Stan:

Who was the first guy you had sex with after your divorce?

Gloria:

Oh – that was Mr. Fling! He lived at my apartment complex. I met him when my living room and dining room were turned into a hut, because instead of fixing a couple of small leaks, the workers managed to make the leaks worse. It was literally raining throughout that entire room. Fling-guy took care of everything. He was extraordinary – coming over immediately – whether it was to clean my furniture, or to install new carpeting. The workers had to build a new roof. I was staying in an empty apartment on the property, while he was repairing my apartment. We came to know each other, and he told me he was contemplating leaving his wife. It had nothing to do with me: he was fed up with the marriage. One night, he called me at about 10:00pm, to ask if he could come over and analyze the situation. He brought his own beer and drank the six-pack, while we discussed the pros and cons of his marriage. Before he left, he hugged me and I kissed him on the cheek. When his wife saw my lipstick, she became hysterical. They talked things over, but he was still contemplating a separation. One night, we decided to go to a Mexican restaurant for drinks. I was flying from two cocktails, but Mr. Fling only had a couple of beers, so I had a much bigger buzz than he did. We went back to my apartment and I was stunned, because the sex was really, really good! This was the first man I had sex with after my divorce. For it to be sexually gratifying and passionate was a momentous revelation! I didn't want to marry him, but I was very fond of Mr. Fling. And he did end up going back to his wife.

Chapter Six

Fake Sex!

Gloria:

Do you want to know what my strangest sexual experience has been?

Stan:

I can't wait to hear this!

Gloria:

I was introduced to Ryan, a man who had been divorced for several years. His wife had been having an affair for a few years, without him knowing about it. She was an accountant, and he thought during tax season, that she must be working nonstop. When he found out about the affair, it ended their marriage.

On our first date, Ryan and I went out for dinner, and neither of us had cocktails. I wasn't feeling well. I couldn't eat my dinner: it may have been the 90-degree heat; I swam for over an hour earlier during the day. The restaurant was too hot, as well. Ryan drove me home after dinner. We parked for a few minutes and he kissed me a few times. At noon the next day, he sent me a text, asking if he could drop by – since he was in the area. I told him I was still sick.

One week later, we went to another restaurant, this time for drinks with appetizers. We both had strong mixed drinks, and I went back to his house with him. We fooled around but we did not have sex. He was about ten years younger than me, but he looked and acted about ten years older. Ryan fell asleep, while I lay awake most of the night. At some point after 6:30am, I finally fell asleep. He woke me up at 11:00am, to say he needed to drive me home because he had work to do. I went into the bathroom to wash up, and when I walked back into the bedroom, he was lying on the bed, naked. He asked me to join him. So I took off my clothes and suddenly he's on top of me, but he isn't inside me. Ryan did not have an erection! Yet, his entire body was going "up and down" and "up and down" and "up and down" ferociously! It was like you'd see in a film – and that's what it felt like – being in a film or a soft porn video. I was wondering: "What the hell is he doing?!" When he finally finished, he put his clothes back on and I did the same. This was "fake sex" as I've never seen it! It was truly beyond comprehension! HE ACTUALLY PRETENDED TO HAVE SEX WITH ME, WHEN HE DIDN'T HAVE AN ERECTION!!! This was the most bizarre sexual encounter I've ever experienced! The most bizarre encounter, period! Stan, one of the reasons I decided to have sex with him was for you and me – to add even more excitement to our affair! I can tell that almost having sex with Ryan has made you jealous!

Stan:

That's true!!! Though if he had really screwed you, it would have been a lot hotter!!!

Gloria:

He thought he screwed me. Doesn't that count for something? And I looked hot. You would have loved the top I wore, since you can unzip it in the front, from top to bottom. I'll send you a photo of what I wore. Stan, why was he pretending that he was inside of me? I don't get that, at all! I don't understand any of this!

Stan:

Unless it was his first time, he would definitely know whether he had an erection or not.

Gloria:

He's psychotic!

Stan:

He hasn't called or sent you a text?

Gloria:

No. I guess it doesn't matter since he's embarrassed. I mean, he had to know.

When I put my clothes back on – my jeans and top were inside out because I undressed so quickly. Then we each had a glass of water – that's all he offered – no juice, no breakfast – just water! I don't remember what we talked about when he was driving me home, since I was so stunned by what had just happened, or didn't happen. This was the most idiosyncratic encounter of my life!

Stan:

You know when you are hard or not hard. If he wasn't hard, he couldn't penetrate you. He had to have known.

Gloria:

Thanks for confirming it! So, he was pretending he was inside of me, like we thought! That makes it even weirder versus just telling me he has trouble getting an erection. He invited me to have sex with him! I wasn't the one lying naked on the bed, waiting for him! Why would he bother to "act" since he didn't have to see me again? That's what's so damn bizarre. Well, I wouldn't go out with him again, in any case. Oh – he did send me one very short text message, but I didn't understand what he was saying. It was Twitter shorthand, and I'm never on Twitter.

Stan:

I am curious as to what he wants!

Gloria:

Then you go out on a date with him, next time! Answer me this: Why didn't he take a pill when he woke up, if he needs an RX for an erection? He let me sleep until 11:00am, so why didn't he take a damn pill? He made the first move at the restaurant. We were sitting across one another at a table outside, and he pulled up a chair, so that he could sit next to me and hold my hand. He talked passionately about his wife's affair. I decided "what the hell" and went back to his house with him. Little did I know what was going to happen... AND, one more thing: he told me that he and his ex-wife had a good sex life the entire time she was having her affair. Now that should have been a red flag, right there!

Chapter Seven

The Sensuality of Gloria and Stan

In this age of virtual reality, people are meeting via dating websites, emails and text messages, FaceTime, and through various apps. We are discussing the most intimate topics with individuals all over the world – with people we have never been introduced to. While it feels safe to communicate in cyberspace, no one is truly protected, and that is both alluring and disconcerting. What if we had scrutinized, as students, the most private details in the lives of our favorite artist or scientist or athlete? Would they still be our heroes? Welcome to the 21st Century...

Gloria to Stan:

You are the only person I know, who is so sensual in every way. You love heterogeneity, separate from intercourse. You adore every part of the female body. I'm loving your erotic and passionate nature! All of this is new for me, with you. XOXOXO

Stan:

I guess I really don't know how other men feel about it. I just think that there is so much fun with variety. I just can't do the same thing each time. **I can explore every part of your gorgeous body.** How were your orgasms the last two nights? XOXOXO

Gloria:

Fantastic! I'm so much more relaxed! I've been stressed due to preparing for the art museum exhibit. I'm excited and nervous, but that's a good combination, since I usually feel those emotions before something outstanding is about to happen. **I've told a close friend just how sizzling our phone calls and emails are; that they can be as seductive as actual sex! Especially, as** we get to know each other, more and more. **The foreplay is so liberating. The build-up: on our iPhones; FaceTime; in my bed. All these emails and the hottest positions. I can't wait for you to be inside of me!** I've had the best sex in the world with my first husband and with a couple of boyfriends, so I didn't expect to enjoy what I'm having with you, at this point in my life. It's not only a much-needed diversion; it's also so much healthier for both of us, in every way. XOXOXO

Stan:

The next time I seduce you, I will take care of you!!! I want my partner to be satisfied and electrified!!! I can't stop thinking about your lips and your body! I can't get my hand away from touching myself!!! I will be making love to every part of your body!!! XOXOXO

Gloria:

I have the **Champagne** in the freezer, waiting for us. We will both be inebriated next time, and not just me. You think this build-up is seductive? It will be nothing compared to inaugurating the most amazing water bed – like you've never experienced. It's going to be phenomenal! XOXOXO

Stan:

Love it, love it, love it!!! Did I mention I love it??!! I thought our intimacy had reached new heights before, but OMG, this little helper we tried out last night took us to the moon!!! All I can say is, prepare for splashdown!!! XOXOXO

Gloria:

It's magnificent! Seriously, **this is the best $28 I have ever spent. We've both fallen in love! It's powerful,** waterproof, rechargeable, and with twelve different patterns. There are low, medium, and high intensities. It has everything you could want in a massager. What more could we ask for?! XOXOXO

STAN:

You are so fucking hot!!! XOXOXO

The Next Day

Stan:

What are you wearing right now? XOXOXO

Gloria:

I have on a long, sleeveless denim dress, that is figure-hugging. It has snaps from top to bottom, so if I suddenly stand up, some of the snaps may pop open. It's also low cut and I don't wear a bra with it. I'll send you a photo! XOXOXO

Stan Looks at the Photo

Gloria:

Would you like to pop open my dress? XOXOXO

Stan:

I want to snap open that dress NOW!!!!!! I can't wait for Little Stan to be inside your luscious lips!!!!!! XOXOXOOXO

Gloria:

Did it occur to you that almost all the men I have been with sexually, didn't want a BJ because the actual sex was so magnificent for them, when they were with me?! I happen to LOVE intercourse and so did they! Honestly – only one man has ever asked me for a BJ – when I was in my early 20s. And that was it! XOXOXO

Stan:

There's nothing better than having great sex with you!!! With all the OTHER women I've slept with, there wasn't anything better than a great BJ!!! XOXOXOXOXO

Gloria:

I've been with men who could last up to two hours during intercourse. There's nothing better than the excitement, pleasure, and intense tingling – from head to toe – from mind-numbing sex! Even if we had non-stop sex all weekend, would you still want a BJ? Don't answer that! XOXOXO

The Next Day

Stan:

Are you thinking about all the men you will meet at the Gallery tonight? XOXOXO

Gloria:

Yes, I am. And it will be interesting if this artist's ceramics sell – it's his first exhibit. So, I'll be observing the people coming to his opening night. Essentially, it's a dress rehearsal for me. Do you think high heels are sexy? XOXOXO

Stan:

I do think high heels have sex appeal!!! My hand is now between my legs!!! Are you going to let a man take advantage of your hot body, tonight? XOXOXO

Gloria:

Perhaps, if I have a drink or two. XOXOXO

Stan:

Are you enjoying my dark side? (LOL!) XOXOXO

Gloria:

It's not dark. We are having FUN. There's nothing wrong with that. I love your "dark side." XOXOXO

Stan:

You have me soooo turned on right now!!! We have come a long way, haven't we, in just a few months!!! **Would you like to have sex with Andy, since he'll be at the Gallery tonight??!!** XOXOXO

Gloria:

He may assume that I will have sex with him, when we finally meet again, but he's into dressing up in costumes and videotaping everything. You have to be demented to make tapes in this day and age. I have no interest in watching myself having sex. XOXOXO

Stan:

I would be turned on, watching a video of you having sex!!! XOXOXO

The Next Day

Gloria:

Good morning. Did you dream about us last night? I was so tired after choosing frames and hanging paintings, that as soon as I went to bed, I fell asleep. XOXOXO

Stan:

I woke up hard, thinking about your hot body!!! I had to take care of myself in the shower!!! XOXOXO

Gloria:

Happy to be of service! XOXOXO

Stan:

Did you have sex with Andy? XOXOXO

Gloria:

His flight didn't get in until midnight, so he never made it to the Gallery. Apparently, he missed an earlier flight. XOXOXO

Stan:

So you talked to him? XOXOXO

Gloria:

Briefly. We are going to have lunch today. XOXOXO

Stan:

Is the lunch foreplay? I can't wait!!! Where are you meeting??!! XOXOXO

Gloria:

At a seafood restaurant. I'm not sure what will happen, so stay tuned! XOXOXO

Later that Day

Stan: Are you back from lunch??!! Are you in bed with Andy??!! Inquiring minds want to know!!! XOXOXO

Gloria:

You're going to need a cold shower! XOXOXO

Stan:

Did you both dress up??!! Are you sending me the tape??!! I can't stand it!!! I need a shower right now!!! XOXOXO

Gloria:

I confiscated his phone and didn't give it back to him until he was leaving. Sorry, but I don't trust Andy with a videotape of us having sex. We drank wine with lunch; he came back to my house; and before I could take off my shoes, we were having sex on my living room couch! XOXOXO

Stan:

OMG!!! I can't take it!!! I am so jealous and turned-on!!! I'm taking off my pants and locking the door!!! I have to see your naked body right now!!! XOXOXO

Gloria:

As long as Little Stan makes an appearance! XOXOXO

Stan:

I want to make you crazy with the new lubricant, as I seduce you with my magical fingers!!! Did I tell you how much I love your breasts???!!! XOXOXO

Gloria:

Only a million times! Did I tell you how much I love that you are twelve years younger than me? So my breasts really turn you on, Stan? They need YOUR MAGICAL FINGERS! And now, you are

wondering if we should have a threesome with Andy. Am I correct to assume that? XOXOXO

Stan: I might be jealous if we had a threesome, but I'm "up" for videotaping!!! XOXOXO

One Week Later

Gloria:

WELCOME HOME!!! I hope you had an enjoyable vacation!!! XOXOXO

Stan:

I am back and I will call you later. I have to attend a meeting, right now. I missed you!!! I can't wait to talk to you!!! XOXOXO

Gloria:

I missed you every hour of every day! I'm so happy you are back! Right now, I'm framing some more paintings for the Gallery. XOXOXO

Two Days Later

Stan:

Send me photos of the clothes you are planning to wear at the Exhibit, for the next few weeks!!! XOXOXO

Gloria:

Do you want to see all my outfits? Here's a photo of my sexy black dress that shows cleavage, has arm slits, along with a leather belt and boots. XOXOXO

Stan: Love it!!! XOXOXO

Gloria takes selfies of several outfits

and sends the photos to Stan.

The Next Day

Gloria:

Did you dream about my outfits last night? XOXOXO

Stan:

You are really getting with the program!!! All these sexy outfits!!! I slept great last night!!! XOXOXO

Gloria:

It was so much fun, trying on these clothes, for you. I wish you could join me at the Gallery for the Opening – or longer – for the two months my paintings will be displayed. I'll be wearing eyeshadow, mascara, and lipstick. You've never seen me with all that make-up on. Don't worry, I'll have someone take photos of me with my paintings. XOXOXO

Stan:

You are so FUCKING HOT!!! I will talk to you tonight, after you come home from the Gallery!!! XOXOXO

Gloria:

If only you could come with me! XOXOXO

Stan:

I want to be there with you!!! I will call you tonight!!! Very, Very late!!! XOXOXO

Two Days Later

Stan:

You are going to have to tell Andy that your attorney is coming to town for a few days, and that we will be tied up all night, in various meetings!!! You will see him only after I leave!!! XOXOXO
Gloria:

I'll be tied up with you, literally! XOXOXO

Stan:

You have me crazy, as usual, as I imagine being inside of you!!! XOXOXO

Gloria:

Are we bringing anyone else to our board meeting? XOXOXO

Stan:

Who do you want to join us? The UPS guy? The grocery delivery guy? The gardener? Do you like the idea of them watching us? Or would you prefer if they joined in? XOXOXO

Gloria:

It's getting funnier and funnier, with all these men, each with his own reality. No one fits in – but we all end up together – some watching and some taking part. XOXOXO

Stan:

Well, now I can't stand up!!! I want to take my tongue right down your cleavage!!!!! Who are you making love to? You are so fucking hot!!!!! HOT, HOT, HOT!!!!! XOXOXO

Gloria:

Sorry – I have to choose more frames for my paintings. Later… XOXOXO

Two Days Later

Gloria:

Good Morning! I was up all night, after returning from the Gallery. I was reading and suddenly it's 3:00am and then 6:00am. I eventually slept a couple of hours, though I had crazy dreams, which I cannot remember, now. XOXOXO

Stan:

Oh boy!!! You need to remember the orgies!!! XOXOXO

Gloria:

You are sooooo bad! You are soooooooooooo bad! XOXOXO

Stan:

You are more interesting and more exciting than anything!!!
XOXOXO

Gloria:

Just make sure you stay limber for me!!! XOXOXO

The Next Day

Gloria:

OK. I finally did it. XOXOXO

Stan:

Answer the door with a towel wrapped around you, and then you
accidentally let it slip??!! XOXOXO

Gloria:

You know I've done that before! You won't believe this: I
experimented and went on a dating website. I didn't join – I just
uploaded some photos and wrote that I "love to walk on the beach."
XOXOXO

Stan:

You are making me CRAZY JEALOUS!!! XOXOXO

Gloria:

I'm investigating this website for my friend's daughter, who is dying to meet new men, but she's afraid to join. She had one bad experience, online. She really wants to meet someone special, so she asked me if I would check it out for her. It's an experiment. XOXOXO

Stan:

Why not use her photos and info about her life? XOXOXO

Gloria:

Because she wants to make sure that it's safe for her to join. I have zero interest in these dating websites, but I agreed to check it out for her. And she's smart because these men are deranged! XOXOXO

Stan:

You know I'm feeling a lot of jealousy!!! I don't want you on these websites!!! XOXOXO

Gloria:

You have nothing to worry about. Every man who contacted me was a con artist.

Door #1 told me that he's in Italy and will be retiring to his Los Angeles house, that's worth $2.7 million. First, he needs a ticket to LA. He was calling from Italy, and the connection was very bad, but he used a U.S. phone number, to make it look like he was phoning from the U.S. He wants to marry me. There's a photo of him with two young girls. I sent the photo to my friend's daughter, and she immediately recognized the photo. Apparently, he's someone famous who works in real estate. So this Italian man is using someone else's photo, saying it's him and his motherless daughters, and calling from a fake U.S. number. After the phone call he messaged me, so I blocked him. Apparently, lonely women respond to this type of guy. They'll fly to Italy or fly that person to the U.S. Can you believe it?

Door #2 told me he's fighting in Afghanistan, but he needs to meet a woman, so that he has something to look forward to. He is deployed there for another two months. It was obviously another con job, since his photos don't even match – he looks like two different people in the photos he uploaded. It's not the same man! I told him to contact me when he returns from the war.

Door #3 was another lunatic, who I could barely understand. He told me he's a U.S. citizen, but he speaks a little French, a little Spanish, and very little English. I couldn't understand anything he was saying.

That's it. I'm done. And so is my friend's daughter! XOXOXO

Stan:

That's amazing. I'm glad you shut the door!!! You probably have to go through fifty losers before meeting one decent guy. XOXOXO

Sex in the 21st Century

Gloria:

The door is locked and bolted! Never to be opened again! Anything can happen, out there in cyberspace! XOXOXO

Later That Evening at 1:00am

Stan:

I am waiting for you to join me in the Jacuzzi!!!!!!!!!!!!!!!! XOXOXO

Gloria:

Is the Champagne on ice? Remember, we're taking it into the Jacuzzi with us. Is your glass full? Let me see! XOXOXO

Stan:

I really missed you!!!!!!!!!!!!!!!!!!!!!! My glass is full!!!!!!!!!!!!!!!!!! XOXOXO

Gloria:

Oh, this is so great! My mind has been racing one thousand miles an hour. **I've been dying to spend time with you!** I feel so much calmer, already. Tell me what you are going to do to me. XOXOXO

Two Days Later

Gloria:

Good morning! **I walked in the rain to the 7/11 to buy a lotto ticket.** I also bought my favorite donut. XOXOXO

Stan:

You could win the wet t-shirt contest!!! XOXOXO

Gloria:

Especially since I didn't wear a bra. XOXOXO

Stan:

That's what I figured! XOXOXO

Gloria:

So tell me about your first time, when you lost your virginity. XOXOXO

Stan:

I started dating at around sixteen years-old. Send me a photo!!! XOXOXO

Gloria:

I'll send you a photo of me in my wet t-shirt! XOXOXO

Gloria Sends the Photo

Stan:

Much better!!!! So hot!!!! I love looking at your cleavage!!!! I want to kiss every part of it!!!! XOXOXO

Gloria:

I'll let you do that! XOXOXO

Stan:

Would you let your favorite athlete **undo your robe and let it slide to the floor?** XOXOXO

Gloria:

Only if we were going to have sex! XOXOXO

Stan:

You are having sex, aren't you? Isn't this leading up to intercourse? XOXOXO
Gloria:

I'll show you tonight what I would do to my favorite athlete! XOXOXO

Stan:

You are so fucking hot!!!!!!!!!!!!!!!!!!!!!!!!! XOXOXO

Gloria:

Happy to entertain you! XOXOXO

Stan:

You are a wonderful entertainer. I think you need the vibrator right now!!! I can't get the picture of you using the vibrator out of my head! I am going to need relief tonight!!! Be ready for me!!! It's going to be a WILD TIME!!! XOXOXOOXO

Gloria:

I save the vibrator for YOU, ME, and MY ATHLETE! XOXOXO

Stan:

I want you tonight!!! XOXOXO

Gloria:

You can have me, tonight! XOXOXO

Stan:

How about every night??!! XOXOXO

Gloria:

I'm yours!

As I ponder our relationship, we keep each other SANE, providing the excitement we are both so desperate for! We intersect with this joie de vivre that most people can only dream of. All my life, I've felt anxious when a man is into me: that I won't be able to do what I want to do; that I won't be able to do what makes me happy. But with you, I feel adored. We've never had one argument, and it's so much fun, sneaking around so our partners don't find out. **Do you remember the first time we talked? It was for about three hours. You told me: "You've lived the way most people want to live their lives but don't!"** When my life becomes exciting again, you will be part of it. We can travel together, since I'll need an attorney, by my side. The travel will be work-related, right? XOXOXO

Stan:

We will need to relieve all your stress caused by work!!! XOXOXO

Gloria:

We'll relieve the stress; that's for sure. We will christen each room of my new condo! You'll be making lots of trips to visit me in LA. XOXOXO

Two Days Later

Stan:

Did you have any wild dreams last night? XOXOXO

Gloria:

I am back! I missed you! How were your dreams, the last couple of nights? XOXOXO

Stan:

I did not have sexy or wild dreams, but I busted out in the shower this morning, just by thinking about you doing all kinds of erotic things to me!!! What were you doing last night? Did anyone turn you on at the Gallery??!! XOXOXO

Gloria:

No. Only you can turn me on!

I forgot to tell you: this new vibrator makes my entire body pulsate, for a few minutes *after* I stop using it. XOXOXO

Stan:

That's why we bought it!!! Worth every dollar!!!

I want you to expand on the context of what you meant by saying: "I am not 'status quo' and neither are most of my friends." XOXOXO

Gloria:

Well, I've moved around a lot, living in major cities, and I quit every job, whenever I was bored. I've lived on both coasts, and I waited a long time to get married. Marriage was never part of my life plan. I've always wanted a thrilling life. That's where I must get back to. Hopefully, this new painting exhibit will be constructive. I'm happiest when I am creative, inspired, and excited by life. That's why this new Gallery Exhibit is pivotal for me.

Now YOU are Mr. Status Quo: You've lived in Cleveland all your life. You are raising 2.5 children in the suburbs; and you've been divorced only once. That makes you "status quo." If you didn't have what you call your "dark side" – you would probably detonate.

While I'm not "status quo," as I reflect upon my life, I am relatively sane compared to other people on the planet. As my life becomes exhilarating again, you will be part of it. You are part of my life now and for forever! XOXOXO

Stan:

I'm imagining making love to you on every part of your body!!! XOXOXO

Gloria:

I'm imagining enjoying it, on every part of my body! XOXOXO

Stan:

I know you are!!! I am having trouble functioning today, thinking about your sensual and gorgeous body, from head to toe!!! XOXOXO

Gloria:

When we are together, tonight, I'm going to wear something very sexy, just FOR YOU! XOXOXO

Stan:

You are always hot!!!!!!!!! I am thinking about making you crazy, so much that you will have non-stop orgasms. XOXOXO

Gloria:

I know you are!!!!!!!!!!!!!!!!!!!!!!!!!!!! I can't wait!!!!!!!!!!!!!!!!!!!! Both of us will have non-stop orgasms!!!!!!!!!!!!!!!!!! XOXOXO

Stan:

I wanted you last night!!!!!!!!!! XOXOXO

Gloria:

You could have had me last night!!!!!!!!!!!! XOXOXO

Stan:

I want you tonight!!!!!!!!!!!! XOXOXO

Gloria:

You can have me tonight!!!!!!! XOXOXO

Stan:

My imagination is running wild!!!!!!!!!!! HOT!!!!!!!!!!!!!!!!!!!!! XOXOXO

Two Days Later

Gloria:

I've determined that you must have a breakfast meeting, once a week, with a high-ranking client – and that client is me! Everyone will be working, except for you and me. We can live out our fantasies!

I've also decided that I'm going to have sex with you in the pool. We could have sex in the deep end, since it's only five feet deep. The security camera doesn't show what you are doing below the water's surface. We could have sex, while it looks like we are simply standing close together, just as people do, when they talk. Even if there are people lying in the sun, they won't be able to see what we are doing. It will be fantastic! I've had sex on boats, in a lake, and in the ocean. So, I know what I am talking about! You will love it – it's a pleasure you have yet to enjoy! You always love it, when I introduce you to new adventures. Just as you've come up with X-rated phone sex; I would never have believed that phone sex could be so provocative and seductive! We work well together, don't you think? And the vibrator was your idea, and it certainly has enhanced our sex lives! XOXOXO

Stan:

I'm all in – the vibrator – the pool – you name it and I'll be there!!! XOXOXO

Three Days Later

Stan:

This has been one crazy week!!! I haven't even talked to you!!!!!!!!!!!!!!!!!! I have been missing you all week. I was imagining you in the shower with me this morning!!! XOXOXO

Gloria:

Were you lathering me up? XOXOXO

Stan:

Yes, and Little Stan was lathered up, too!!! I'm going to call you in one hour, so I hope you are available!!! I want to wish you an early HAPPY BIRTHDAY!!! XOXOXO

Gloria:

If you are steamy and sensual, I am available! XOXOXO

Stan:

We are so HOT!!! XOXOXO

Gloria:

We are concurrently incredibly and incredulously HOT! I'm going to tantalize you with photos of my seductive short shorts. I'm sending the photos, right now! Can you imagine the two of us on our own private island, with me only wearing these sexy shorts? It would be so alluring! We will swing it – in LA – as we have discussed! XOXOXO

One Day Later

Stan:

I am getting hard looking at those photos!!! I want to see you on all fours in those shorts! XOXOXOOXO

Gloria:

After I've had a bottle of Champagne on ice!!! XOXOXOOXO

Stan:

Start drinking!!! XOXOXOOXO I want you to only have the shorts on and nothing else!!! XOXOXOOXO

Gloria:

OK – that sounds like fun! I'm so easy it's ridiculous! It's like a film, isn't it? X-rated? XOXOXOOXO

Stan:

Isn't all sex X-rated? I am thinking about taking those sexy short shorts off of you!!! Would you like to be videotaped? So, you think you are easy? XOXOXOOXO

Gloria:

With you I am!

These are crazy cool short shorts! Keep dreaming about them while I dream about you: EVERY INCH OF YOU!! I love that we can be erotic and psychotic together! XOXOXOOXO

Stan:

OMG!!! You make me crazy!!!!!!!!!!!!!!!!!!!!!!!!!!!!!!!!!!!! I LOVE IT WHEN YOU ARE CRAZY. WHEN WE BOTH ARE CRAZY LIKE TODAY!!!!!!!!!!!!!!!!! HOT HOT HOT PANTS!!!!!!!!!!!!!!!!!!!!!!!!!! XOXOXOXOXOXO

Gloria:

I will wear SEXY SEXY SEXY OUTFITS JUST FOR YOU!!!!!!!!!!!!!!!!!!!! XOXOXOOXOXOXOOOXOXOXOOXO XOXOO

Stan: LOL; you are so fucking hot!!!!!!!!!!!!!!!!!!!! Now I am going to be looking at you in these shorts all week!!! I won't be able to work for the rest of this week!!! For the rest of this month!!! XOXOXOXOXOXOXOXO

Two Hours Later

Gloria:

You have to choose a day, when you can make love to me in the pool. There are a few old men who sit under an umbrella playing cards. They will not be peering at us; I can assure you of that. XOXOXO

Stan:

My hand is between my legs, playing! I am excited about men looking at you and getting hard in their bathing suits. I imagine you flirting with them, checking out their bodies, making me crazy!!! XOXOXO

Gloria:

They are not watching me because they are too busy with their card game. I only see them when I'm walking to or from the pool.

So here's our swimming pool plan: If you are too nervous to have sex in the pool, we can use the pool as foreplay. Little Stan will be turned on, and you and I will be turned on! After swimming, we will come back to my apartment, soaking wet! I'll invite you into my bed and we will have wild and frenzied sex! XOXOXO

Stan:

I'm Coming Over NOW!!! XOXOXO

Gloria:

I Can't Wait! XOXOXO

Two Days Later

Stan:

I am so turned on thinking about your body and making love to every part of it!!! I want to make the sex sooooo fucking hot for you!!! I want you to feel every inch of me inside you!!! XOXOXO

Gloria:

I am so turned on – reading your emails and imagining my responses. This is the most erotic and arousing foreplay: I start visualizing and it writes itself! You are my muse, and I am yours. Who knows where these emails will take us to: Long Island Ice Teas, sexy outfits, whipped cream, positions for the most intense orgasms – the build-up to all of this. With our imaginations and the hot sex we both long for, next Monday is going to write itself! XOXOXO

Three Days Later

Stan:

I heard your message about the accident!!! Thank goodness you are OK!!! Can your car be repaired? Are you driving a rental? Or are you using Uber? I need to hear more about the cop!!! I love your ideas!!! Is it the cop's uniform; the hat; or his power??? Are you getting as turned on as I am??? OMG!!! OMG!!! OMG!!! I can't wait to see your emails tomorrow!!! XOXOXO

The Next Day

Gloria:

It's everything about the cop! He is such an aphrodisiac! He's very good looking – probably in his late 30s – a little younger than you. What do you think about a threesome?! XOXOXO

Stan:

Hot, Hot, Hot!!!!

Better looking than me??!! That's OK!!!! I know what pleases you!!!! You want us both, don't you? He will make it so much fun!!! The three of us. Wow!!!! I can see it: wild and crazy!!!! XOXOXOOXO

Gloria:

I am sooooooo turned on by the cop: thinking, imagining, and talking to you about him. This is the most stimulating and lustful foreplay. **I am laughing, just thinking about us with my cop!** XOXOXOOXO

Stan:

I am thinking about your lips and your body and the cop!!! **This foreplay is so fucking hot!!! I want to kiss every part of your body!!!** I will be making love to every part of your body, while he watches!!!!! I am going crazy thinking about you, me, and the cop!!!!!!!!! It is probably a good thing I changed my staff meeting until next week, so we can spend time with the cop!!!!!!!!! I have my priorities straight, don't I????!!!! XOXOXO

Gloria:

Perhaps I just had my affair with the cop – visualizing him with you and me! Now it seems improbable, that I will see my cop again, because I've told you what I've been thinking/feeling since the accident. I was sitting in the back seat of his car, for what seemed like at least an hour, since he had to take a few phone calls. Then he drove me to the car rental agency, and he even came in with me. He didn't leave until they pulled up with my rental car. He's great looking and caring! Why didn't I give him my business card? I am so turned on, dreaming about him and imagining this affair with you! AND YOU ARE JUST SO CRAZY – LOVING ALL OF THIS! It doesn't matter that my car was totaled! It was worth it!

Perhaps I'll see him in court, if I don't pay the ticket. I guess he could always contact me. You, me, and my cop! My lust! Your fantasies! Does it get any better??!! XOXOXO

One Day Later

Stan:

I have been thinking about you screwing other men!!! I dreamt that you were sleeping with other men!!! I can't stand the thought of you with other men!!! I am trying to make time for you tomorrow. How about the beach??!! XOXOXO

Gloria:

You see, almost having sex with the cop has made you jealous! It's great for our relationship. I'm available today, tomorrow, and for

the rest of the year, for YOU! It sounds like you had some passionate dreams last night?! Let's make love on the sand as the waves crash onto the beach, "From Here to Eternity..." XOXOXOOXO

Stan:

Oh yeah!!! Between the heat, the orgasms, and the long day at the beach, it will put both of us to sleep!!! I love having this affair with your cop, even if it turns out to be a fantasy. It is so much fun when we let ourselves go. We had a spectacular release, taking care of both of our needs???!!!

Your attraction to other men turns me on and on!!! Remember, having sex with both of us at the same time is really just a fantasy. If it turns you on, you need to just go with it!!! Maybe you will think of the two of us when you want to play!!! If it turns you on, you can think of him when you are with me!!! Everything should be on the menu when we fantasize!!! XOXOXOOXO

Gloria:

The menu keeps expanding and it's tasting spectacularly good. If I sell enough paintings, I'll be able to buy that penthouse condo. XOXOXO

Stan:

You deserve the penthouse!!! I am imagining making love to you right now, on the roof of that penthouse!!! XOXOXO

Gloria:

We'll make love in the salt water pool, on the roof of my penthouse. Did I tell you about that? That's one of my dreams, having a pool across from my living room in that penthouse. XOXOXO

Stan:

You have a love affair with water. Swimming in the ocean. Swimming in any water!!! You have needs that must be satisfied!!! You can't only just make beautiful paintings!!! XOXOXO

One Day Later

Gloria:

Swimming is very sensual. It's what I have introduced to you: swimming in the pool at 3:00am. I'm sending you a photo of me in my new purple bathing suit! Meanwhile, there's another man in my life: Ben, my new assistant. He is talking like he's falling in love with me. He's imagining a new life with me. He's married, but that doesn't seem to matter. XOXOXO

Stan:

OMG!!! You are so hot in that bathing suit!!!!!! Your gorgeous cleavage!!!!!! I want to let your breasts spill out into my face. I want to lubricate your entire body. XOXOXO

Gloria:

I'll let you do that! XOXOXO

Stan:

You are so hot!!!!!! **I can't take it!!!!!!** Who are you making love to, in that sexy purple bathing suit photo??? It's not Ben, is it??? HOT, HOT, HOT!!!!!!!!!!!!!!!!!!!!!!!!!

Well, now I can't stand up!!! You are so fucking hot!!! I need to take another cold shower!!! I have been thinking about playing with those bathing suit straps, while kissing your neck!!! **I want to kiss every part of your body! What's Ben look like??!! OMG!!! I'm starting to get jealous again!!! Does he turn you on??!! OMG!!! XOXOXO**

Gloria:

NOOOOOOO. Here's what he just sent me:

"The only thing on my mind is our great new life with two beautiful people."

Stan: "WTF??!!" He is talking about love and commitment? Does he know that I come along with the package? LOL. XOXOXO

Gloria:

NOOOOOOO. He doesn't need to know that you service me in more ways than one! XOXOXO

Stan:

I just love the way you say that!!! I just love to service you!!! I love to fulfill all your needs!!! XOXOXO

Gloria:

Ben will do anything I want him to do, so I can handle the situation, as of now. I don't want him to be obsessed. I told him yesterday that he needs to initial the contract. Here's what he wrote:

"Once I sign, we are together for the next two months. Since you will be selling all of your paintings, we'll be making more beautiful paintings. We'll be together forever. I love it."

Ben sent me another email late last night: "You have given me a new life. I was going through the motions – at home and at work. You have brought me back to life." So, he's fallen in love... UGH... XOXOXO

Stan:

His love for you is turning me on!!! I have a lot of movement going on!!! **XOXOXO**

Gloria:

You always have movement going on with me! XOXOXO

Stan:

You are right; I can't help it! I have my hand between my legs!!! You have needs that must be satisfied!!! XOXOXO

Two Days Later

Stan:

What's Ben look like? XOXOXO

Gloria:

Ben is "okay" looking. He's got long hair, but he doesn't turn me on. He looks like an aging hippie. This "falling in love" stuff is rather annoying when it's every day, every hour. I need him to calm down and concentrate on his work and not on me! XOXOXO

Stan:

He has you for two months (LOL!), and then I get you back??!! Is that how long the Gallery showing is? XOXOXO

Gloria:

Two months or when I sell my last painting; whatever comes first. You will always have me... We will always have Paris... **I could feel you inside me last night. OMG!** XOXOXO

Stan:

Oooohhhhh. I thought we accomplished a lot last night (LOL)!!! Remember, I had originally said we may have to choose between dinner, showering, and lovemaking. We did two out of three!!! We were not interrupted for a very long time. I'm going to have to drink some coke to stay awake, but it was worth every minute, making love to you!!! XOXOXO

Gloria:

If only you could put me to sleep at 3:00am every night, without waking up your kids. **I think we could fall asleep in each other's arms, don't you?** Ben woke me this morning, with an early phone call that wasn't necessary. I forgot to turn my phone off. You see what I mean, when I say he's exasperating? I'm starting to get irritated at the mere thought of him! **XOXOXO**

Stan:

Just keep Ben in his place!!! You only have room for me!!! I have to assume Ben has never been with anyone who has your looks. No wonder he's in love!!! Do you think he would trade in his wife to be with you? OMG!!! XOXOXO

Gloria:

Ben wishes he had been with me from the beginning, living the life I have lived. He's never felt he belonged in his conventional life. He had a few good years with his art – he makes fantastic pottery – but you know my life has not been easy and he would have never survived it. He is like a child: he is play-acting. He's a pretend rebel and a half-hearted artist. Enough about Ben! I finally feel that everything is falling into place, and you are part of it. XOXOXO

Stan:

I am excited!!! It is like I said. Everything seems to be lining up for you, finally!!! And, you deserve all the upcoming success that you have worked so hard to get!!! I am always happy to lighten your load!!! It's always very hot!!! I love servicing you!!! I can't get enough of it!!! XOXOXO

Are Emails Hotter Than Sex

Gloria:

Dream of me tonight or in the shower tomorrow morning. And then come over for a swim. I have everything you need except for shorts! XOXOXO

Stan:

I don't need shorts!!! Skinny dipping!!! XOXOXO

Gloria:

So you will be caught on the security camera? What would happen to you then? They can't see us having sex in the pool, but they will see your nude body jumping into the pool. I'll have to bail you out of jail! I'll have to take out money from my secret funds! XOXOXO

Stan:

What an adventure!!! We should do it!!! XOXOXO

Gloria:

We will skinny dip at my new condo. Dream about that! XOXOXO

Two Days Later, Gloria sends Stan

New Photos of Her Outfits

Stan:

Love, love, love the photos!!! Nice!!! You are looking so hot!!! The men will be out-bidding one another to buy your paintings, just to be near you!!! XOXOXO

Gloria:

I want them to love my paintings! I don't want them to love me! So you approve of my outfits: the sexy tops with the faux leather skirts? I'm even letting you choose my clothes, for God's sake! XOXOXO

Stan:

I love choosing your clothes for you!!! We have a wonderful relationship!!! There shouldn't be boundaries, other than when I exceed your comfort levels!!! XOXOXO

Gloria:

I agree! We have telepathy, sensuality, AND sex in the pool! We have too much fun! XOXOXO

Stan:

You know how to make my day!!!! You look great!!!! Love the cleavage!!!! XOXOXO

Gloria:

I had to display the cleavage! I know what you want! XOXOXO

Stan:

I am excited about these men looking at you tonight and tomorrow night and for another two months!!!!!! I'm imagining you flirting with them and checking out their bodies. It's making me crazy!!!!!! I was thinking about who would buy you a drink and who would turn you on???!!! I've been trying to work and I suddenly realized

I was tired – and – oh yeah – it's the Champagne I drank with you late last night!!! But I feel good!!! Are you tired, too? You were amazing!!! I am having so much trouble working today!!! I can't stop thinking about you and all these men!!! I'd love to come to the Gallery and watch, but these men would make me so jealous. I know I wouldn't be able to stand it!!! XOXOXO

Gloria:

Ben is going to videotape the Gallery Opening tonight, so you have that to anticipate! No one will know that we are lovers: you are always in my vault! Except when you are protecting my copyright, with this book on my paintings. I'm attaching the contract with this email, so go back to work! Wish me luck, tonight! I love you!!! XOXOXO

Stan:

I love you, too!!! I'm going to contact you later, before you leave for the Gallery. XOXOXO

Glorla:

About the contract? XOXOXO

Stan:

Yes. And I'm also going to "ROCK N ROLL INSIDE YOU!!!" XOXOXOOXOXOXOOXOXOXO

Gloria:

OMG!!

XOXOXOOXOXOXOOXOXOXO

Chapter Eight

Good Night

Gloria:

This was our fantasy affair – communicating via iPhones, FaceTime, photos, and our imaginations – to keep this romance alive and provocative. Our liaison was titillating, intoxicating, and always filled with joy. We have not met and we may never meet. The most extraordinary revelation, is that our sex lives with our partners are exciting again. If that's not vindication for an email affair of the heart, I don't know what is!

Blue Danube Publishing

Elaine Feuer is the CEO of Blue Danube Publishing. In 2018, Elaine co-wrote: *Chaya's Angels: A Spiritual Journey with Down Syndrome* **with Chaya Ben Baruch. When Chaya gave birth to her sixth child, a son with Down syndrome, she led her family on a spiritual journey, moving from Alaska to Israel, and adopting more children with special needs, on the way. Whether she's watching her son with Downs marry her adopted daughter with Downs, or fighting for the rights of all special needs children, life is never dull. Chaya even managed to find time to donate a kidney, leaving everyone to wonder, "What's next?" Ghandi wrote: "A nation's greatness is measured by how it treats its weakest." Join Chaya and her family on their enchanting odyssey. The world needs this heartrending story, more than ever!**

Elaine's book, *Traveling In and Out of Heaven,* **is the story of her brother's five month battle against esophageal cancer, encompassing: the profound love between a brother and sister as they struggle with the torment of an unbearable illness; the love and support of family and friends; and the treacherous betrayal of a daughter. The poignant and agonizing issues in this narrative are circumstances that readers could encounter at some point in their lifetime: an unsigned medical proxy; next-of-kin power over medical decisions; life support; and a duplicitous legal petition. Once you start reading, you won't be able to stop!**

Elaine began contemplating end-of-life issues after witnessing her mother's slow and painful death from cancer. *To Gently Leave This Life: The Right To Die*, is the perfect reference book for the grassroots activist, legislator, and for people who are dealing with their own or a loved one's terminal illness. It is Elaine's aspiration that medical aid in dying will be approved throughout the U.S. and in countries across the globe. Whenever possible, people deserve the right to have a 'gentle and happy' death.

Blue Danube published an enthralling memoir, *The Last Waltz: Love, Death & Betrayal* by Professor Sean Davison, and edited by Elaine Feuer. In 2006, Sean cared for his terminally ill mother, Pat Ferguson (a psychiatrist), during the final three months of her life. The Last Waltz is the story of an extraordinary love between a mother and son, and how their informed decisions lead to unforeseen consequences: A sister betrays her brother; a son is charged with murder; Archbishop Desmond Tutu requests bail, igniting a public debate about voluntary euthanasia and the right-to-die. In 2018, Sean was arrested for helping three men in unbearable pain, to die. His punishment is three years of House Arrest in Cape Town, South Africa.

Elaine wrote the critically acclaimed exposé, *Innocent Casualties: The FDA's War Against Humanity* – which is now available in its fourth edition as an eBook: Irene Alleger, editor for Townsend Letter for Doctors & Patients wrote: "Innocent Casualties manages to make the blood boil in righteous anger, because it makes the FDA's abuse of power so personal... Ms. Feuer takes the reader step-by-step through the nonsensical tactics, deceit, and police mentality."

Elaine has worked in the medical division of Little, Brown & Company and freelanced as a research and development coordinator for a variety of film and television projects, including the critically acclaimed films, Imagine: John Lennon; 25 x 5: The Continuing Adventure of the Rolling Stones; Elvis: The Great Performances; Learned Pigs & Fireproof Women. Elaine obtained history and criminal law degrees – "Graduating With Distinction" – from the University of Toronto; received "Academic Excellence in Editing" from the University of Massachusetts; and was an "Ontario Scholar."

www.ingramcontent.com/pod-product-compliance
Lightning Source LLC
Chambersburg PA
CBHW071346130626
46556CB00005B/2051